Little Bear Goes to Kindergarten

Jutta Langreuter and Vera Sobat

The Millbrook Press
Brookfield, Connecticut

For my mother Kata, with all my love.
V. S.

"Good morning, Little Bear," said Mama Bear. "This is a wonderful day—your first day of kindergarten. Did you remember?"

"I remember," said Little Bear.

Mama said, "I made you a honey sandwich for lunch. You're going to eat with your new friends, remember?" asked Mama.
"I remember," said Little Bear.

"Are you going to bring Teddy, Little Bear?
I think it would be OK today but you'll have to remember
where you leave him so we'll be able to bring him back home."
"Boy," said Little Bear, "it's good I can remember so much."

On their way to school, they passed the park. Little Bear waved to Oscar on the swing.

"I remember there's a new playground at my school," said Little Bear.

"That's right," said Mama, "and there are swings and slides just like these."

Little Bear stopped to pet a puppy.
"I remember we're going to have a rabbit at school," said
Little Bear.
"Won't that be neat?" said Mama.

When they got to school Little Bear remembered where
his room was, and there was his teacher.

"I remember you from when we came for a visit," said Little Bear.

Ms. Brown said, "I remember you, too, Little Bear. I'm so glad
you're here."

"Little Bear, I want
you to meet the other children in the class. Here are Betty,
Danny, Nicole, and Brandon. Can everyone say hello to Little Bear?"

All the children shouted a big "Hi!" and Little Bear smiled and said "Hi" right back. Then he looked around for Mama.

"I'm right here," said Mama Bear. "But you need to pay attention to your teacher now, not me."

Just then Ms. Brown came to get Little Bear. "Will you come with me to see the rest of our classroom, Little Bear? I've got so much to show you."

"I remember this!" shouted Little Bear, and he ran to the slide.
"That's right, Little Bear," said Mama Bear. "Now I remember,
too. You liked that slide when you came to visit before school
started."

"We've got some new things, too," said
Ms. Brown. "We have plants to take care of, sponges for the
blackboard and nice, clean clothes for the doll corner. And next week
we'll get our rabbit! Now, will everybody take a place at the art table,
please?"

Little Bear looked around for his mother and saw her standing by the door. "Don't go, Mama."

"I need to go soon, Little Bear. Paint a picture for me."

Little Bear liked to paint. He could see that the other children liked painting, too.

A few minutes later Little Bear ran over to his mother.
"Look, Mama! I painted a picture of you!"
"That's wonderful, Little Bear. Make me another one and when
I come back we'll take them both home to show Papa."

"But I want to come with you now," said Little Bear. Then he whispered, "Will you ask the teacher if I can take the picture now?"

Ms. Brown said, "Come and wash up, Little Bear. We are going to mix up a special snack with yogurt and raisins and oatmeal."

"But I have a honey sandwich," said Little Bear.

"You can eat that, too," said Ms. Brown, "but come mix with us."

Little Bear joined in the mixing, and they made a wonderful snack.
"Here," said Little Bear to his mother, "try some!"
"Mmm, it's good," said Mama, "and that reminds me. I've got to do my shopping now."

Little Bear was watching Mama leave as Ms. Brown was saying, "Who wants to play cops and robbers?"

Everybody shouted at once, "I want to be a cop!" and, "I want to be a robber!" Nicole said, "I want to be a princess!" Little Bear said...

"I want my mother!"
Mama Bear didn't know what to do, and neither did Ms. Brown.

Brandon Bear came over and took Little Bear by the hand.
"Come on!" he said. "Be a robber with me. I know the best place to hide."

As the other children started to count, Brandon and Little Bear ran off to hide and Mama slipped out the door.

When Mama came back just before the end of kindergarten, the children were playing blindfold tag.

She watched them play for a while and she could hear Little Bear laughing.

Mama called out, "I remembered to come back to school to get someone but I don't remember who!"

"Mama!" shouted Little Bear. "It's me! You remembered me."
"Oh, yes," said Mama Bear, "my Little Bear! It's time to go now."

"Wait, Mama," said Little Bear. "There's something I forgot."

Mama watched as Little Bear ran to the secret hideout and said, "Goodbye, Brandon. I'm going to remember you all the way until tomorrow!"

"Me, too," said Brandon. "See you tomorrow!"

First published in the United States of America in 1997 by
The Millbrook Press, Inc., 2 Old New Milford Road,
Brookfield, Connecticut 06804

English language text copyright © 1997 The Millbrook Press

Copyright © 1995 arsEdition GmbH, Friedrichstrasse 9,
80801 Munich, Germany

Langreuter, Jutta.
[Kleine Bär kommt in der Kindergarten. English]
Little Bear goes to kindergarten / Jutta Langreuter;
[illustrated by Vera Sobat].
p. cm.
Summary: Little Bear likes the teacher, other children, and
activities on his first day at kindergarten, but he does not
want his mother to leave.
ISBN 0-7613-0191-7 (lib. bdg.)   ISBN 0-7613-0231-X (pbk.)
[1. First day of school—Fiction. 2. Kindergarten—Fiction.
3. Schools—Fiction. I. Sobat, Vera, ill. II. Title.
PZ7.L2695Lf 1997
[E]—dc20   96-35112   CIP   AC

3 5 4   (lib. bdg.)
3 5 4 2 (pbk.)

Printed in Italy